Acting Edition

T0284264

The Lights Are On

by Owen Panettieri

‖ SAMUEL FRENCH ‖

FOR PRODUCTION INQUIRIES

UNITED STATES AND CANADA
info@concordtheatricals.com
1-866-979-0447

UNITED KINGDOM AND EUROPE
licensing@concordtheatricals.co.uk
020-7054-7298

Each title is subject to availability from Concord Theatricals Corp., depending upon country of performance. Please be aware that *THE LIGHTS ARE ON* may not be licensed by Concord Theatricals Corp. in your territory. Professional and amateur producers should contact the nearest Concord Theatricals Corp. office or licensing partner to verify availability.

THE LIGHTS ARE ON received its world premiere on October 13, 2023, at Theatre Row in New York City, produced by New Light Theater Project and Embeleco Unlimited. The production was directed by Sarah Norris, with scenic design by Brian Dudkiewicz, costume design by Kara Branch, lighting design by Kelley Shih, and sound design by The Roly Polys (Jan Bentley & Andy Evan Cohen). The Property Master was Danielle Pecchioli, the Wardrobe Supervisor was Krista Grevas, the Master Electrician/Assistant LD was Hayley Garcia Parnell and the Technical Directors were ToniAnne and Jordan Cavanaugh. The Producing Associate was Kleo Mitrokostas, with casting by Gamma Valle and press representation by Charlie Guadano. The Production Stage Manager was Josh Blye. The Assistant Stage Managers were Jessica Kemp and Hugo Wehe. The House Managers were Caroline Mack and Sam Tuschinski. The cast was as follows:

LIZ	Danielle Ferland
TRISH	Jenny Bacon
NATHAN	Marquis Rodriguez
LIZ/TRISH UNDERSTUDY	Carolyn Baeumler
NATHAN UNDERSTUDY	Hugo Wehe

CHARACTERS

LIZ – Disaster supply enthusiast, widow, 40s/50s, Female.

TRISH – Comes from wealth, divorced, 40s/50s, Female.

NATHAN – Liz's gay adult son, Relationship status: it's complicated, 20s, Male.

While Liz and Trish can be played by actresses of any race/ethnicity, it is the playwright's original intent that Nathan be portrayed by an artist of color that does not physically resemble his mother. Nathan looks like his father, whose race/ethnicity is never expressly stated.

SETTING

A Suburban Ranch House.

TIME

A Little Further On From Now.

AUTHOR'S NOTES

My journey with *The Lights Are On* started in 2017. At the time, it felt like we were living in a world of perpetual chaos and instability, and I wanted to explore the sense of anxiety and isolation people were experiencing at the time. And this was pre-pandemic! We had no idea what was coming around the corner. Many people are still experiencing a high level of anxiety, manifested in new ways. We strive to connect with our family members and with our neighbors, while navigating what often feels like fractured realities. Forget about having differences of opinions; people can't even agree on the same set of facts on which to base those opinions. The act of disagreeing and the embrace of distrust seem to be more important than facing our collective challenges.

The world of *The Lights Are On* is a little bit further down the road from us. Liz, Trish and Nathan find themselves having to determine whether everything around them is as it seems or if nothing is as it seems. I have great compassion for Liz, Trish and Nathan. They are funny, deep-feeling fighters who unfortunately lie to themselves even more than they do to each other – or to the audience. Are the roots of their grievances truly as they remember them? I'm excited for audiences to go on this journey with them and to reach their own conclusions as to who and what on stage can be trusted.

I think there is a lot of room for interpretation with the design elements of the play, including the representation of the Grey Man, who is not a listed character, but certainly has a presence in the show. In our premiere production, he was physicalized as a shrouded figure portrayed by our assistant stage manager, Hugo Wehe. In terms of costumes, there is again room for interpretation, but the choice of Nathan appearing in a jockstrap when he briefly changes clothes onstage is intentional and meant to convey his comfort with his sexual power as a queer person.

This play is dedicated to KC, always inspiring.

First Escalation

(A suburban ranch-style house. We can see the kitchen/eat-in dining area, back door entrance, and a hallway leading to the rest of the house. It looks like the kitchen you might have once seen in a 90s sitcom, that could now benefit from a modern facelift. If you didn't look too closely, it wouldn't seem so bad. In truth, this heart-of-the-house is a diseased organ. While it is not a disaster area, someone here is planning for disasters. Storage containers and cardboard boxes are stacked high in corners. An old portable radio sits on top of one box, turned off. Cleaning supplies are stockpiled around and under the sink, paper towels and toilet paper fill the space above the cabinets. Folded laundry is piled neatly in a basket on a chair by the kitchen table. There is a chessboard on the table, with red and white armies ready for battle. Heavy-duty gas masks have recently arrived in the mail and sit in an unmarked box on the floor. By the wall nearest the table is a shelving unit where a 9mm handgun rests, unsecured, on top of more traditional kitchen items. Battery-powered lanterns line the room, should the electricity fail. Blackout curtains are drawn on the kitchen's only window. The back door is adorned with multiple locks. LIZ, a middle-aged woman, stands at the kitchen peninsula, going through a large plastic bin holding emergency food supplies. She is

dressed casually, without shoes. She inspects the expiration dates on the canned food. If the date is far off, it goes back in the bin. If not, it goes in a pile for the cupboard. She enjoys this task. There are piles of batteries, bottled water, and first aid materials on the counters. As **LIZ** *sorts, she hums a happy tune. There is a quick knock at the back door.* **LIZ** *stops. She's left the latch off the door, expecting her son. Another knock, quicker, longer.* **LIZ** *looks toward the gun, but decides not to go for it. A third quick knock.* **LIZ** *stands, picks up a knife from the counter, goes to the door and quickly latches it.)*

TRISH. *(Offstage.)* Oh, Liz. Please, if you're there. Come to the door!

*(**LIZ** recognizes the voice. She is baffled by who must be standing at her doorstep. It's someone she hasn't seen in years. She peeks through the peep hole.)*

LIZ. *Trish?*

TRISH. Oh, thank god! Please open up!

*(**LIZ** takes a breath, unlocks the door and opens it to reveal **TRISH**, a woman of Liz's age, dressed fashionably, breathing as if she just ran for a distance. She looks at **LIZ**, and seeing her, loses her nerve and smiles.)*

Hi, *neighbor*! How are you?

LIZ. I'm fine.

TRISH. Good! Good... I know it's late. I'm embarrassed to be doing this, but –

LIZ. What's wrong?

TRISH. Can you come with me for a minute?

LIZ. Outside?

TRISH. I need to show you something. Just down the driveway. It'll only take a minute.

LIZ. Why? What is it?

TRISH. It's easier if I show you. Would you just come with me to the end of your driveway?

LIZ. Trish, you don't look right...

TRISH. Please?

LIZ. I have nothing on my feet!

TRISH. Just slip on whatever's closest.

LIZ. Stop and explain to me what's wrong. Is someone hurt?

(*With rising dread.*) Is it *Nathan*?

TRISH. Oh, no no! I didn't mean to scare you like that.

LIZ. Did someone hurt *you*?

TRISH. No. But I think someone might be planning to...

> (**LIZ** *considers* **TRISH** *for a moment. She can't imagine what would bring* **TRISH** *over here, but likes the idea of being the bigger person.*)

LIZ. Come inside. Come on.

> (**TRISH** *enters.* **LIZ** *shuts and locks the door without the latch. The lights flicker.* **TRISH** *notices it, but* **LIZ** *does not.*)

TRISH. Oh, it's nice and warm in here!

LIZ. Well, I've got food on the stove.

> (*There is, in fact, no food on the stove. A pie is baking in the oven.* **LIZ** *puts the knife back on the counter.*)

TRISH. It got cold out tonight. I'm sorry to barge in on you –

LIZ. Just tell me what's happened. You can say it. It's just you and me.

TRISH. I need you to come look at my house.

LIZ. Why?

TRISH. I was driving home from seeing my sister. I'd been out most of the day, and as I turned the corner onto our block I saw...the lights are on in my house.

LIZ. All of them?

TRISH. No. Just one on the second floor. The one in my bedroom.

LIZ. Okay, so?

TRISH. So I never leave that light on when I go out, Liz.

LIZ. Oh, you just didn't notice it was on because the sun was up when you left your house!

TRISH. No! I mean, *maybe,* but –

LIZ. That's all it took to get you this wound up?

TRISH. No... I think someone was looking out at me from my bedroom window. It was a silhouette. Behind the curtain. The shape of a body, I think.

(**LIZ** *laughs it off. Typical Trish!*)

LIZ. Trish, it's probably nothing!

TRISH. That's why I want you to tell me if I'm being crazy or if it really looks like someone –

LIZ. I can't leave right now.

TRISH. You won't have a look with me?

LIZ. I've got food on the stove, Nathan's not home yet –

TRISH. It'll take two minutes.

LIZ. If it's *nothing*, two minutes. But if it *is* something –

TRISH. So you do think it could be something?

LIZ. Did you set your alarm when you went out?

TRISH. Of course!

LIZ. Then I'm sure it's nothing. Why don't you sit for a minute? You want some iced tea?

> (**LIZ** *goes to the fridge without waiting for an answer, pulls out an open bottle of white wine.*)

TRISH. I don't want to be trouble.

LIZ. Yeah, well. Excuse the state of the house. It's chore day, so now I'm halfway through everything and finished with nothing.

> (*She gets a mug from the drying rack by the sink.*)

TRISH. It's fine. I really am sorry to bother you with this. I know this must seem –

LIZ. That's why we have neighbors, right? Heh. To think, after all this time, *this* is what finally gets you down that hill and back over here. Drink this.

> (**LIZ** *hands* **TRISH** *the mug of wine.*)

TRISH. It's just that when I drove up and saw the light on in the upstairs window... I couldn't make myself turn into the driveway. I had to keep going. And then I saw your light on –

LIZ. From the street?

> (*This seems like a physical impossibility to* **LIZ**. *She checks how much light could be spilling out from the window.*)

TRISH. Yeah! And I thought, "Let me check with Liz. She'll tell me if I'm being crazy."

LIZ. You're being crazy.

TRISH. Am I?

LIZ. I think it's much more likely you left your light on without realizing it. You're letting yourself be scared about nothing.

TRISH. If I just had someone to walk back with me so I didn't feel so –

LIZ. I'm in for the night. You can stay here as long as you need until your bad feeling passes.

TRISH. Where's Nathan tonight that you're still expecting him?

LIZ. I asked him to go to the store after work. I'm restocking this thing.

TRISH. Where's he working now?

LIZ. A pool supplies store. Out in Helen's Bay.

TRISH. Oh! That's a nice area. Heck of a drive from here though.

LIZ. That's where they were hiring. He doesn't mind. And the pay's not bad for his age, so… He should be home any minute.

TRISH. Oh! Would you call him?

LIZ. Why?

TRISH. He could look at my house as he drives by to see if there's someone in the upstairs window.

LIZ. He's not allowed to use his phone while driving.

TRISH. And you think he follows that? He's technically an adult now. I'm sure he does what he wants.

LIZ. That's the rule.

TRISH. You put a lot of trust in him.

LIZ. I do. Did you lock up your car?

> (**TRISH** *takes a sip of her wine.*)

TRISH. When?

LIZ. Before you came up to the house. Did you forget and leave it unlocked?

TRISH. No, I locked it.

> (*Or did she?* **TRISH** *shifts uncomfortably.* **LIZ** *notices.*)

LIZ. Do you keep a gun in the car?

> (**TRISH** *laughs nervously.*)

TRISH. Liz!

LIZ. Well, do you?

TRISH. No, I don't drive with a gun in the car.

> (*Or does she?*)

LIZ. Plenty of people do.

TRISH. Well, not me! Do you?

LIZ. I avoid driving altogether, if I can help it.

TRISH. But when you do?

LIZ. Depends on where I'm heading.

TRISH. Would you let *Nathan* drive with a gun in the car?

LIZ. Of course not! Could you imagine if he got stopped for something and they found a gun on him?

> (**TRISH** *takes a sip from her cup.*)

TRISH. Where is it now?

LIZ. My car? Nathan has it.

TRISH. No, your gun!

LIZ. Locked up and that's where it's staying. I am *not* lending it to you.

TRISH. I wasn't asking you to!

LIZ. You're too jumpy. You'd shoot at anything that moved right now.

TRISH. I don't want a gun. I just want someone to take a look at my house with me. You know, if there's someone over there robbing me, they could just as easily come over here next.

LIZ. Heh. No one's getting in over here.

TRISH. What would stop them?

LIZ. They'd be making a big mistake to try. I'll tell you that. Try and relax, will you? Do you mind if I go back to straightening some of this stuff out?

TRISH. No, of course.

> (**LIZ** *goes back to sorting.* **TRISH** *looks around.*)

Your place looks nice.

LIZ. Trish, it's obvious the house is a mess. There's no need to tell me otherwise.

TRISH. I meant...you've changed some things up! I haven't been over in a while, I guess.

LIZ. Seven years. Not since Joe's funeral.

TRISH. Not *that* long.

LIZ. Name another time since.

> (**TRISH** *thinks. She cannot remember a more recent time.*)

TRISH. That was a difficult day. But a nice remembrance.

LIZ. I mostly remember how quiet it was.

> *(This is a pointed statement from **LIZ**, but **TRISH** does not acknowledge it.)*

TRISH. This furniture's different now, yes?

LIZ. We had to replace a lot of it after the flooding from Prudence.

TRISH. Can you believe it'll be the five-year anniversary of Hurricane Prudence this Saturday? When you can remember the date a storm hit, you know it was a monster.

LIZ. No way to forget that one. Afterwards, there wasn't a lot worth saving. It all had to go.

> *(**TRISH** sits at the table and watches **LIZ** repack the emergency food.)*

TRISH. Are you alright, Liz?

LIZ. Me? I'm fine. Why?

TRISH. I feel like we used to talk all the time and now I'm realizing just how long it's been.

LIZ. Life gets busy for everybody.

TRISH. It's tough living on your own, huh?

LIZ. I'm not on my own. I have Nathan.

TRISH. I meant without Joe.

LIZ. It's hard at times, but we're used to it.

(Feeling obligated to ask.) And you? How are you?

TRISH. It's been rough lately. I don't like living alone. I wasn't built for it. I mean, obviously! Look at me. I'm scared to go home by myself.

LIZ. Have you heard from Richard lately?

TRISH. Only through his lawyer. Which is sort of fine. His lawyer's always been very nice to me. He's kind. He has a kind voice for a lawyer.

> (**LIZ** *softens a bit toward* **TRISH** *and moves toward her.*)

LIZ. If someone was robbing your house, do you really think they'd sit and wait by your window? Wouldn't it be more likely they'd hide someplace, so you didn't know? Then they could jump out at you when you weren't suspecting or – you know, I meant for this to be reassuring, and it completely got away from me somehow, but you get what I mean.

TRISH. That's just the thing. When I looked up and saw that figure in the window, I felt like he *wanted* me to see him. He *wanted* me to know he was waiting. It felt like he was pleased with himself that he'd gotten in and he was claiming my house as his space. He was daring me to enter.

LIZ. You felt all that just as you were pulling up to your house?

TRISH. Yes. Immediately. All at once.

LIZ. Do you want to call the police?

TRISH. No, I don't want to involve them. I don't need them in my house. They'll turn the place upside down and then I'll have to try to put it together again on my own.

LIZ. Yeah, you're better off handling it yourself.

> (**LIZ** *gets up and goes back to repacking the food.*)

TRISH. Can we watch some TV? That might calm me down.

LIZ. Well, I got rid of cable.

TRISH. You did?

LIZ. I was sick of paying for it. And sick of watching it, quite frankly. It's all garbage lately. Especially the news.

TRISH. Oh, I can't stomach the news.

> (**TRISH** *starts to play herself at chess. She is sitting at the white side but gradually starts losing to the moves she is making against herself as red.*)

LIZ. But it was really the cost. My monthly bill used to be an already-insane $140 for cable and internet. Well, last month they had that merger, and Trionics became Meglamax, you know? So I look at my new bill. It's $230 for the month. For the same service!

TRISH. No!

LIZ. Mmhmm. So I call them up and this *lady*, starts trying to gaslight me about the new price in this disgustingly saccharine tone –

TRISH. Ugh, I hate that fake nice tone!

LIZ. Oh, I know! And I say to Miss Meglabitch, "No. This bill is insane. I'm dropping the cable. Just leave me the internet," because Nathan would lose his mind without the internet, and there's no other service in town. And I tell you, it feels so much better to be done with it. You don't realize how much time you waste sitting there in front of a screen, sucked in.

TRISH. Outstanding! And Nathan doesn't mind?

LIZ. He minds, but he's still got his computer and his phone. He can watch stuff that way.

TRISH. That's true. And that's not the same thing, right? It's different! Different...screens!

LIZ. Yeah! You feeling better? You're looking better. Let me get you some more tea.

(**LIZ** *takes the mug from* **TRISH** *and brings it back to the fridge. She refills it with white wine.*)

TRISH. I think you gave me wine.

LIZ. Yes, of course, wine. That's what I said.

(*They give each other a look, but* **TRISH** *lets it go.*)

TRISH. I have my cable bill on auto-pay. I haven't even thought about how much I'm spending on it. It's probably the same situation as yours.

LIZ. Yeah, but you can afford it no problem, right?

TRISH. But it's the principle of it!

LIZ. So look into it.

TRISH. I will. I'll look into my sister's too.

LIZ. (*With veiled skepticism.*) Which sister is this now?

TRISH. Gladys. You met her a while back. She lives twenty minutes away now, out in Memmorack.

LIZ. Oh. How is she?

TRISH. Not great. The last few years, she's been having major mobility issues. It's not easy.

LIZ. I'm sorry to hear that... Gladys is the one you had that big falling out with, right?

TRISH. Over my mom's estate. You remember that?

LIZ. Oh, sure! You were pissed.

TRISH. I was! And we didn't speak for years. But when her health started to go, she reached out again, and I'm so glad she did. These past few years have been really healing for us. Still, she can't do much for herself and I'm the only family she has left, so a lot falls on me. I spent the whole day over there just cleaning.

LIZ. That does sound like a lot.

> *(This story does not match up with what* **LIZ**
> *remembers about* **TRISH** *and her sister, but*
> *she is not ready to call* **TRISH** *out on it.* **LIZ**
> *wants to see* **TRISH**'s *whole show.)*

TRISH. It is. I'm trying to convince her to move in with
me. I mean, I've got nothing but space. But she doesn't
want to give up her house. I can't blame her. It's her
home. I wouldn't want to give up my house.

LIZ. Provided you can bring yourself to go back inside of it
at some point.

TRISH. You make fun, but have you ever had your house
broken into before?

LIZ. No.

TRISH. Well, let me tell you – it's the *worst*.

LIZ. Wait, you've had this happen before?

TRISH. Yes!

LIZ. In *that house*? When?

TRISH. No, it was before we moved here. Richard and I
had a house up in Everly. A cute little ranch-style. A
little bit like yours, actually. I'll never forget – we'd
been out all day at a wedding. I'd just found out I was
pregnant a few days before, and we were both over the
moon. So we pull into the driveway that night, and...
I just knew. Richard and I *both* knew. Something was
off. Sure enough, someone had broken in through our
back porch.

LIZ. You're kidding! What did they walk away with?

TRISH. No theft. They just came in and smashed everything.
From our wedding china down to the bathroom mirrors
– they trashed the entire house. We never found who
did it either. Could've been one person. Could've been a
group. Cops came up with nothing.

LIZ. That's terrible!

TRISH. It was. I had all these little hand-painted porcelain figurines that my mother gave me. A friend of hers used to make them, and my mom helped her with the orders. They were beautiful. I had them all set out in a glass display cabinet. Whoever broke in stomped on every single one. The clean up took forever. We tried to make a go of it there after, but with Jeremy on the way? I could never relax thinking about it. So we moved here.

LIZ. I had no idea! Did any of your neighbors have the same thing hap–

TRISH. No, it was just us.

LIZ. Well, that seems very targeted. Did the police question –

TRISH. You're missing my point. I *know* that feeling when something's not right. I've lived through it before. And as I drove up to my house just now, it was so... I cannot go through it again. I had Richard with me back then. I have nobody now. I can't walk into my house and see it vandalized, defiled, and with someone still waiting –

> (**LIZ** *grabs the red king from the board and lies him down in checkmate. The overhead light flickers. Only* **TRISH** *notices.*)

LIZ. Trish, you just left the lights on.

Second Escalation

> (*The sound of keys in the door.* **NATHAN**, *a man in his early twenties, enters wearing a shirt that says "Poolside." He carries a heavy bag of groceries in his arms and has an extra set of keys in his hand.*)

NATHAN. Mom?

LIZ. Here, sweetie! Let me help you with that. *Trish* has stopped by.

TRISH. Hello, Nathan. Look at you! It's been a while!

NATHAN. Yeah, hi... Is everything alright?

(*He hands* **LIZ** *the groceries.*)

LIZ. We're just catching up.

(**NATHAN** *looks* **TRISH** *over. He's got questions.*)

NATHAN. Um, I saw your car outside. You left your door open.

TRISH. I did?

NATHAN. Yeah, you did.

(*He kicks his shoes off by the door.*)

LIZ. Trish, you said you locked it!

TRISH. I thought I had. I mustn't have closed it hard enough when I got out.

NATHAN. It was the front *passenger* door that was open.

TRISH. The *passenger* door?

NATHAN. Yeah, I closed it for you. You left the keys inside too. Here.

(*He hands* **TRISH** *her car keys. She is flustered.*)

TRISH. Thank you.

NATHAN. You're sure everything's okay? Is there –

LIZ. We're fine. Trish had a bit of a scare earlier, but things have calmed down and we just got to talking.

(**NATHAN** *gives his mom a look.*)

Is that so surprising? Moms swap stories!

NATHAN. Some moms do.

LIZ. Don't be fresh. Did you find everything on the list?

NATHAN. Yeah, they actually had everything tonight.

LIZ. That's a nice change! And no one gave you any trouble? No one –

NATHAN. I was *fine*. It was okay out there tonight.

LIZ. You're later than I expected.

NATHAN. There was a bunch of outstanding paperwork I wanted to get done at the store, so I stayed late to finish it.

TRISH. Nathan, you didn't happen to notice if I left the lights on in my house while you were driving home, did you?

NATHAN. No, I came down from the opposite direction. I saw your car on the side of the street ahead of me as I pulled up to the house.

TRISH. Would you mind –

LIZ. Let's let Nathan get settled in first, Trish. He's had a long day.

NATHAN. Pie smells good. You put it in when I said?

LIZ. Yes, it's in the oven. Almost done.

TRISH. You're baking?

LIZ. I told you I had a pie in the oven.

TRISH. You said, "Food on the stove."

LIZ. You can smell it, can't you?

TRISH. Oh. Yes…

(**TRISH** *sniffs the air. She can't smell the pie.*)

LIZ. In this house, pies are a team effort. Nathan makes 'em. Mom bakes 'em. Sweetie, if you want to take a shower, you've got time before it's ready.

NATHAN. No, I just want to get out of these clothes.

LIZ. There's fresh laundry over there.

NATHAN. Okay.

> (**NATHAN** *walks over and picks out shorts and a top.* **LIZ** *puts the bag down in the kitchen and starts taking out cans of food and inspecting them.*)

TRISH. Nathan, your mom tells me you're working at a pool supplies store in Helen's Bay.

NATHAN. That's right.

> (**NATHAN** *takes off his shirt and drops it on the floor.*)

TRISH. Is it busy this time of year?

NATHAN. Very.

TRISH. Really? It's not off-season yet?

NATHAN. It should be. People don't seem to be treating it that way.

> (**NATHAN** *unbuckles his pants and pulls them off, revealing he is wearing a sexy jockstrap.* **TRISH** *is surprised by his lack of modesty and looks away while trying to maintain the conversation.* **NATHAN** *puts on his shirt and shorts. He exhibits no embarrassment about changing in front of* **TRISH**, *or being seen in such intimate underwear. He dives into his pants pocket for his phone. Turns it on.*)

TRISH. And you'll work there all year?

NATHAN. That's the plan.

TRISH. What do they do in the winter? Do they have to reduce staff?

NATHAN. I don't know. This is my first season at the store.

TRISH. Well I guess it's always summer someplace, right? Maybe they do online orders!

NATHAN. Maybe. Still feels like summer here. It's been over eighty and humid all week.

TRISH. It's chilly tonight.

NATHAN. If we had a pool, I'd go swimming right now.

TRISH. Really? Working around pool stuff all day doesn't make you sick of it?

NATHAN. No. Swimming's always made me feel good.

> *(They smile awkwardly, but sincerely, and then* **NATHAN** *turns his attention to his phone. His smile fades.)*

TRISH. Well, you're looking really great.

NATHAN. Yeah. If you don't mind, I have to...

> *(He turns away, focusing on typing a message.)*

TRISH. Liz, can I help you with anything in there?

LIZ. No, I've got it. You relax.

TRISH. You sure? Okay...

> *(She takes a long sip from her mug. Finishing, she turns back to* **NATHAN.***)*

So, do you guys sell those big pool floats? The ones shaped like swans and unicorns? I saw on TV those were very popular this year.

NATHAN. We sell them. They're cool.

TRISH. They're so big! The toys and things weren't so creative when I kept my pool up. We had those gray rectangular rafts! Remember? Mine had a cup holder. I thought that was a wonder at the time. Now they're these *creatures*!

NATHAN. You had that alligator too. I liked that one.

TRISH. Oh, I guess we did!

NATHAN. I just saw the catalog with the ones coming next year. There's this one company that makes them. Next year's theme is, "Monsters of The Sea."

TRISH. Monsters? Oh that's funny!

NATHAN. They're pretty dope. There's a Loch Ness Monster, a creepy crab, a giant squid –

TRISH. Oh, a squid! I don't like those. I wouldn't want to float around on that!

*(**LIZ** perks up at hearing this.)*

NATHAN. Really?

TRISH. Nope. Not for me. They're awful.

LIZ. You don't eat fried squid?

TRISH. No! I think about those little suction cups on the legs-arms-ugh!

LIZ. Richard used to serve calamari all the time at your parties.

TRISH. I know, but I never ate it. He did it to torture me!

NATHAN. The squid raft is cool. The head is sort of in the middle of it and the legs raise up and create the back and the sides. It's like a throne.

TRISH. To think of looking out my window and seeing a giant squid floating around in my pool! No way.

NATHAN. Lots of people have it on pre-order.

TRISH. People are crazy... So you're all done with school now, I assume?

NATHAN. School's done with me.

LIZ. Do you want a beer, honey?

NATHAN. Okay.

> (**LIZ** *gets a bottle of soda from the fridge.*
> *A timer rings.*)

LIZ. That's the pie!

> (*She takes it out of the oven and sets it on the*
> *stove.*)

TRISH. Maybe I should be going.

LIZ. No. Stay for pie. *We're happy to share.*

NATHAN. It still needs to cool, Mom. That's another hour
or so –

LIZ. You like eating it hot.

> (**LIZ** *hands him the soda.*)

TRISH. You made it, huh? That's impressive!

NATHAN. Not from scratch. It's pre-made ingredients.
I just mix 'em together.

LIZ. It always tastes better than it should the way he does it.

NATHAN. Fresh stuff would be better, but where you
gonna get it, right?

> (**NATHAN** *takes a swig of his soda.*)

TRISH. Right... well it should cool. I'll go. Nathan, would
you mind walking me back to my car?

NATHAN. Down the driveway?

TRISH. It's dark. I'm a little on edge tonight.

LIZ. Tell you what: You stay for pie and he'll walk you all
the way home after.

TRISH. But I'm sure you both have –

LIZ. C'mon, Trish. Stay. Let's really catch up.

TRISH. Sure. Okay.

> (**NATHAN** *gives* **LIZ** *a look, but has his own shit to deal with on his phone. He puts the soda down on the counter and sits at the table as* **LIZ** *goes back to work at the peninsula.* **TRISH** *stands between them.)*

LIZ. Doesn't Trish look nice today, Nathan? You'd think she was coming straight from Sunday services!

TRISH. Ha! Maybe I do look like that in this.

LIZ. I haven't gone to mass in a long time. Do you know who's the pastor there now? Is it still Father Mateo?

TRISH. Oh, no. It *has* been a long time for you if Mateo was still there. No, he was reassigned a few years back. Which was too bad. I liked him.

LIZ. They didn't give it to Father Daniel, did they?

TRISH. No. Father Daniel got reassigned too. There isn't a permanent pastor right now.

LIZ. I never liked Father Daniel. I always found his eulogies were so self-serving.

TRISH. You thought his *eulogies* were self-serving?

LIZ. No, not "eulogies." What word am I looking for?

NATHAN. *Homilies.*

LIZ. That's right! The homilies. I just couldn't – You remember how he'd never sing with the choir at mass? He'd sing his own song every week, but never include them.

NATHAN. Because they were terrible and he wanted to sound good.

LIZ. Yes, it was more important that he sound good than it was for him to connect with the faithful in the room. I just thought, "Why am I sitting here listening to this guy?" So we stopped going.

NATHAN. We stopped going after Dad's funeral.

LIZ. Well, that was another Father Daniel debacle! Calling Joe by the wrong name for half the service. He keeps going on about how "John" was this and "John" was that. I thought he was talking about the Apostle John, until I figured out he didn't know Joe's name.

TRISH. He knew Joe's name, it was a slip of the tongue. He didn't realize what he was saying.

LIZ. I don't get it. You're an active member of a community for twenty years. You show up week after week. You put money in the collection plate – and we did! No matter what we were struggling with, Joe always felt there were less fortunate people who needed it. Then he dies, and when it's time to say goodbye, the guy behind the altar doesn't have the slightest idea who he is. If they can't get that moment right, what's the point of any of it?

TRISH. I don't know.

LIZ. Me neither... Is Sister Prudence still there? She was a good lady.

TRISH. She was lovely. She passed away a few years ago.

LIZ. Oh, I'm sad to hear that. She was the opposite of Father Daniel. So thoughtful. Nathan, you remember when she used to give you and Jeremy those giant chocolate chip cookies after youth group? She kept them in the fridge to keep them cold?

NATHAN. Yup. She was nice.

TRISH. One of the last times I spoke to her she was annoyed that Hurricane Prudence had her name and did so much damage in the community she served. I think people joked with her about it, not really knowing that it bothered her.

LIZ. Aww. God bless, Sister Prue.

(**LIZ** *puts the soda back in the fridge.* **NATHAN** *types into his phone.*)

TRISH. Who've you been typing away to?

NATHAN. His name's Austin.

TRISH. Is he a friend?

NATHAN. My boyfriend.

TRISH. Oh, what's he saying?

NATHAN. Nothing. *I'm* writing to *him*.

TRISH. But what's he saying back?

NATHAN. Nothing.

TRISH. You've been writing to him since you got home and he hasn't said one thing?

NATHAN. We're kind of in a fight. I am telling him how I feel.

LIZ. Tell him to come over!

NATHAN. Are we hosting a party now?

LIZ. If I want to. I haven't seen him all week. He's *handsome,* Trish.

TRISH. Oh, is he?

NATHAN. *Mom...*

LIZ. I think so. But too many piercings.

NATHAN. STAAP.

LIZ. Just my opinion. His face doesn't need all that hardware.

(**TRISH** *leans in to* **NATHAN.**)

TRISH. It's his body, so what's the harm. Right?

NATHAN. Well, he's got a couple in places that *do* require extra consideration.

   (**TRISH** *leans away and takes a big drink from her mug.*)

LIZ. Invite him over. Sorting things out face to face is better.

NATHAN. He can't drive at night.

TRISH. I don't blame him. I don't like driving at night either.

NATHAN. Well, he *can't*.

LIZ. You're gonna keep being rude, you can hand the phone over and I'll turn it off.

NATHAN. It's my phone!

LIZ. It's my house.

TRISH. He wasn't rude. I was just being too nosy. Type your message. Let me make myself useful. How can I help with this stuff, Liz?

LIZ. Don't trouble yourself.

TRISH. No, really!

LIZ. Well, those four cans can go in the top cupboard over there.

TRISH. Got it.

   (**TRISH** *takes the cans over to the cupboard, pulls on the handle but it won't open. The handle is on the wrong edge of the door. She runs her hand along the bottom until it opens the opposite way. She is disturbed by this, but stacks the cans on the shelf.*)

LIZ. So how's Jeremy doing? You hear from him recently?

TRISH. Um, not for a little while. But he's good. I figure I'd hear otherwise.

LIZ. Did he start grad school right after college?

   (**TRISH** *has no idea.*)

TRISH. When I think about the daily battles to get him to do his homework after school and now he's after all these degrees...

LIZ. They've come a long way from playing G.I. Joe in the backyard. Right, Nathan?

NATHAN. Yup. We've come so far.

LIZ. Remember that summer the big tree fell and you two turned it into your own jungle gym before Dad cut it up for firewood?

NATHAN. Well, we didn't have a swing set, so we improvised.

TRISH. *We* had a swing set!

NATHAN. Not 'til after. Jeremy cried when the tree got chopped up and then you bought him one.

TRISH. That's right. That thing took up way more space that I thought it would.

NATHAN. And then you got rid of that and put in the pool.

TRISH. The evolution of a backyard. Your kids get older and the toys get bigger.

NATHAN. Not our yard. Tool shed. Garden. Grass.

LIZ. Barbecue. Patio. Slip 'N Slide. You had plenty of fun back there.

TRISH. You know your mom had quite the green thumb. She grew the best tomatoes in your backyard. I remember.

LIZ. Yeah, back in the day.

TRISH. You don't keep the garden now, do you?

LIZ. Oh, no. I wouldn't eat whatever grows back there now. With the new stuff they started spraying to kill the mosquitos?

(She snaps the lid on the tub.)

This one's done.

(She starts to drag it to the hallway.)

TRISH. I'll take a side.

LIZ. Sit and relax. I'm just taking it to the closet to switch it with the next.

> (**LIZ** *drags the container offstage.* **TRISH** *walks over to* **NATHAN** *at the table.)*

Third Escalation

TRISH. Your mom and dad used to host the best cookouts. Do you still grill out there?

NATHAN. Dad was the grill master, so...no.

TRISH. I can't believe it's been so long since I've seen your mom. She looks good! You'd think we'd run into each other on the street or at the store or –

NATHAN. Well, she doesn't go outside.

TRISH. What?

NATHAN. She hasn't been out of the house in years.

TRISH. You're joking. That can't be.

NATHAN. It is.

TRISH. When did that start?

NATHAN. I dunno. Over time, she went out less and less. Then she'd only go out to get the mail, or sit on the patio, but I don't think she's even done that in years. She just sits inside all day.

TRISH. That's terrible. Nathan, you have to get her help!

NATHAN. I do help. I bring her whatever she needs.

TRISH. No, professional help.

NATHAN. With all the money I make at *Poolside*? Yeah, okay.

TRISH. I'm serious.

NATHAN. You should go before we have the pie.

TRISH. If you would just walk with –

> (**LIZ** *drags a new container into the kitchen. This one is filled with first aid supplies.* **LIZ** *has her hair pulled back differently, and she is wearing shoes and a necklace.*)

That's more food?

LIZ. No. First aid.

> (**LIZ** *removes the lid and goes to get new supplies from the counter.*)

TRISH. Do you really think you'll need this much stuff?

LIZ. Anything can happen. It's not a lot of one thing. It's a little of everything.

> (**TRISH** *picks up several packs of sealed needles.*)

TRISH. But needles? What are these for?

LIZ. I saw a good deal for them online. You never know.

> (**LIZ** *takes the needles out of* **TRISH**'s *hands, settles them back in the bin.*)

TRISH. Well...the packaging is pretty! You're certainly ready for anything.

LIZ. I try to be. And some of this stuff is valuable and you can make a good profit reselling online.

TRISH. Really?

LIZ. Oh sure. I mean, I'm not trying to price gouge anyone. I'm actually helping people get things they need that are no longer out there.

NATHAN. Mom's mark-ups are always very reasonable.

LIZ. It's an easy work-from-home business.

TRISH. I was just telling Nathan it's so funny how long it's been since we've seen each other. How we haven't even run into each other.

LIZ. Yeah, that's something. Did you tell him yet about the man you think might be waiting in your house?

NATHAN. What?

TRISH. We hadn't discussed –

NATHAN. So *that's* why you want me to –

TRISH. It might be nothing, but –

LIZ. I've been telling her it's nothing.

TRISH. If I left my lights on, I certainly didn't mean to.

NATHAN. Why not? That's the smart move. You leave a light on so people think you're home. If someone's looking to break in, they'd go for a house that's dark and looks empty.

TRISH. I always thought that having your lights on at night made you more of a target. You're drawing attention. That house is still occupied. There's probably something worth taking.

NATHAN. Lights out seems more vulnerable to me.

TRISH. But there are so many empty houses around here lately.

LIZ. There aren't empty houses!

TRISH. There are! You must see them when you're driving around. Foreclosures. Boarded up windows. People just pick up and leave.

LIZ. Where do they go?

TRISH. I don't know.

LIZ. Nathan?

NATHAN. Yeah, there's a couple around.

> (**LIZ** *doesn't like hearing this. She looks at* **TRISH**.)

LIZ. You want another glass?

TRISH. Yes. Maybe you should just leave the bottle out. Save yourself more trips.

> (**LIZ** *takes the mug and goes to the fridge.*)

LIZ. So a few people leave. New people come in. No big deal.

TRISH. The more abandoned houses there are, the more our lived-in homes become targets. There's no way around that.

NATHAN. I don't know. Looting wasn't a major problem after Hurricane Prudence, and we didn't have power for weeks.

TRISH. It wasn't out that long.

LIZ. Yes it was. Almost three weeks we didn't have electricity. They forgot about us. Like they always do.

TRISH. The *clean up* took weeks, but the power –

> (**LIZ** *pours more wine for* **TRISH**.)

LIZ. You had a generator. So you don't remember it being as bad as it was, but it was. And as I recall, you were less concerned about leaving your lights on at night back then.

> (**LIZ** *hands* **TRISH** *the mug and bottle, goes back to work.*)

TRISH. Where did you two stay in the meantime?

LIZ. Here.

TRISH. No! You didn't relocate?

LIZ. Where were we gonna go?

NATHAN. We got by.

LIZ. Yeah. We went to work cleaning up. Junked what couldn't be saved. Fixed our home. No one came around to offer help and we weren't gonna go around begging.

TRISH. I was just next –

NATHAN. You know my mom's a very independent-minded person. Wouldn't ever want to impose.

> (**NATHAN** *gives* **LIZ** *a look. He does not want her to go down this path.* **LIZ** *changes course. For now.)*

LIZ. Anyway, now I know how to plan for the next disaster. Whatever it is.

NATHAN. All we're missing at this point are some, "I Survived the Nuclear Winter" t-shirts.

LIZ. I've got them on pre-order.

NATHAN. Sweet.

LIZ. So, are you inviting Austin over, or not?

NATHAN. The house is a mess. I'm not inviting him over when it looks like this.

LIZ. Well, put your stuff away. That'll be a step in the right direction.

> (**NATHAN** *gets up, picks up his work clothes from the floor and exits through the hallway.)*

TRISH. He's a good kid.

LIZ. I know.

TRISH. You did a good job with him. He's getting to look so much like Joe!

LIZ. You think so?

TRISH. You don't see it? Do you know what the problem is between him and his boyfriend?

LIZ. I'm sure it's not that deep, it's just dramatic. They're young. I mean, the world certainly doesn't make it any easier on them. But they're fine.

TRISH. You like him?

LIZ. Yeah, he's sweet. They're building something nice together. I'm happy for him!

TRISH. Do you let Austin stay over?

LIZ. He has.

TRISH. Is that weird?

LIZ. Yes, a little. But Nathan's an adult. This is his home.

TRISH. I used to worry what I'd do if Jeremy ever told me he was bringing a girlfriend home from college with him, but since he lives with his father –

LIZ. Do you think Richard lets him?

TRISH. Oh, I'm sure. I mean, it's fine! It's just hard to think of your kids as adults. You know?

> (**NATHAN** *re-enters, typing into his phone. He wears a slightly different t-shirt from the one he exited wearing.*)

LIZ. He was always looser about rules.

NATHAN. Hmm?

LIZ. We were talking about who we think is less strict – me with you or Richard with Jeremy.

NATHAN. Oh. You're more strict. By a mile.

LIZ. Ha! Is that so?

NATHAN. Definitely.

TRISH. Have you talked to Jeremy recently? Do you guys keep in touch?

NATHAN. We did, but I haven't heard from him since he went on his social media break.

TRISH. He hasn't been posting?

NATHAN. Uh, he deactivated all his accounts.

TRISH. Why would he do that?

NATHAN. I don't know. It gets exhausting. People get… exhausting.

TRISH. But there wasn't a problem?

NATHAN. He didn't give a reason. At least not that I saw.

LIZ. I think it's a good sign. It means he has stuff he wants to focus on instead of worrying about whatever nonsense people are saying.

NATHAN. Oh! Maybe it's Jeremy that's at your house.

TRISH. What?

NATHAN. Maybe he came home to visit?

TRISH. It's much more likely that I left my lights on.

NATHAN. Why?

LIZ. Yeah. Maybe it *is* Jeremy.

TRISH. No, he'd call. He knows I don't like surprises.

> (**TRISH** *smiles to cover her fear of Jeremy waiting for her.*)

LIZ. Well, first aid stocked. On to the next!

> (**LIZ** *exits, pulling the container back into the hallway.*)

TRISH. Your mom's a piece of work with those bins.

NATHAN. You don't need to tell me.

TRISH. She told me she likes Austin! That she thinks he's sweet.

NATHAN. Why do you keep bringing up Austin?

TRISH. I'm not. I'm just –

NATHAN. Look, the truth is Austin doesn't think people should live like this. He doesn't think you should have three year's worth of food and medical supplies stored in every closet of your home. He doesn't want to be stuck in a decaying neighborhood, he's ready to leave, and he wants me to go with him. But I have her. And she can't go. So neither can I.

TRISH. Have you talked to her –

NATHAN. Are you nuts? I'm not talking to her about any of this.

TRISH. She doesn't expect you to live with her your entire life, Nathan.

NATHAN. No?

TRISH. No.

NATHAN. And who's gonna take care of her? She's gonna be good with you checking in on her once every ten years?

TRISH. I'm just saying it's worth you two talking about it.

NATHAN. Learn to talk to your own family before telling me how I should handle mine.

> (**NATHAN** *picks up the laundry basket and exits to the hallway.* **TRISH** *refills her mug of wine. The light above the table flickers.* **TRISH** *eyes it suspiciously. She checks to see if anyone is coming back in the room, then stands, watching the lamp flicker. It turns an odd color. She notices the gun. She picks it up,*

but holding it frightens her and she puts it down. She flicks the switch for the light back and forth, but it won't change back. **TRISH** *starts to panic. The light suddenly restores on its own.* **LIZ** *drags another container back into the kitchen, wearing a headband and different accessories. This one is filled with flashlights, batteries and disaster gear.)*

Fourth Escalation

LIZ. You feeling alright?

TRISH. Mmhmm. You should have someone come in to check your wiring.

LIZ. Was it blinking again? What we really need is to go on one of those home makeover shows where they gut everything and rebuild it fancy. Wouldn't that be nice?

TRISH. Oh, yes! That would be fun! You should apply!

LIZ. I was kidding.

TRISH. This place isn't so far gone, anyway. It just needs a little maintenance.

LIZ. Don't we all?

> *(They chuckle and relax.* **TRISH** *takes* **LIZ***'s hand.)*

TRISH. We stopped making time for each other. That was a mistake. Coming over tonight, I see that now. But I want it to change. I want us to spend more time together.

LIZ. You've always been welcome over here.

TRISH. I know, but not just that. We should go out and do things together. Make a regular schedule of it. What do you say?

LIZ. Sure. Let's plan on it. Could you hand me those masks?

(**TRISH** *goes and picks up the gas masks. The sight of them makes her nervous. She doesn't want to handle them.*)

TRISH. You think Jeremy's alright, right?

LIZ. Hmm?

TRISH. Nathan said he shut down all his accounts.

LIZ. I'm sure that's no big deal. If it worries you, just ask him about it.

TRISH. I can't just ask him.

LIZ. You're his mother. What's stopping you?

TRISH. Well, the last time we spoke, I said some things in anger that I'm not proud of.

LIZ. Like what?

(**LIZ** *takes the masks from* **TRISH** *and puts them in the bin.*)

TRISH. It's not – I was upset about Richard leaving. I should put it in that context. I mean, I was blindsided by it, and angry. So when Jeremy said he was going with him... well, I really flew off the handle.

LIZ. We all say and do things in the heat of the moment that we come to regret. Family needs to forgive family.

TRISH. I don't know if he will. I was...quite unkind.

LIZ. What did you say to him?

TRISH. I don't...

(**TRISH** *waves her off. She doesn't want to say it.*)

LIZ. So you two haven't spoken since he moved out? But that was –

TRISH. It's been a long time.

LIZ. You have to call him. Whatever it was, just apologize.

TRISH. I don't have his number. His phone was on my account and I canceled it the day he left. I thought that would force him to come back even just to yell at me about it, but he never did. Richard probably just got him a new one. Mom's got no pull. Problem solved.

LIZ. You should reach out to him through Richard's lawyer –

TRISH. No –

LIZ. You said before he's been kind to you. He could help –

TRISH. I told Jeremy he was dead to me. I said that to my son. I started with other things. Cruel things. I finished it off with, "You're dead to me." And now he is.

LIZ. He doesn't think that you –

TRISH. He does.

LIZ. You're his mother. You have to try to make it right.

TRISH. It's funny. Richard and I got married right out of college, and had Jeremy right away, because I had this idea that as a young mom, I'd still be able to remember what being young felt like as my child grew up. I thought I'd be able to relate better, but we never really related. We weren't constantly at each other's throats, but we just didn't understand each other. And now? Maybe the best thing to do now is to just be apart.

> (**NATHAN** *re-enters. Again his shirt and shorts are slightly different from before.* **TRISH** *refills her mug of wine.*)

LIZ. Are you putting those clothes away, or just putting them in piles on your bed?

NATHAN. I'm putting them away.

LIZ. And Austin's coming over?

NATHAN. I asked. I haven't heard back.

LIZ. *Did* you ask?

NATHAN. Mom, please?

LIZ. How are the batteries in the lanterns in your room?

NATHAN. They're fine.

LIZ. Let me go double check them.

NATHAN. Whatever you need to do. You'll see the clothes are put away.

> (**LIZ** *takes a package of batteries and heads offstage.*)

Fifth Escalation

TRISH. She cares! It's a blessing to have someone that cares like that in your life. It really is.

> (**NATHAN** *sees* **TRISH**'s *anxiety.*)

NATHAN. It doesn't surprise me that you're scared up in that house all alone. It's too big to be up there by yourself. I'm never alone here and sometimes it still feels like too much empty space. That probably sounds stupid…

TRISH. Any home can feel empty if someone's missing.

NATHAN. Yeah.

TRISH. Nathan, do you have Jeremy's new number? Not the one he had when he lived here. The one he got afterward?

NATHAN. Yeah. Why?

> (**TRISH** *chickens out. She can't ask for it.*)

TRISH. I was just going to offer it, in case you didn't have it. If you wanted it.

NATHAN. Oh. Well, thanks. I've got it.

TRISH. Good! And you'll let me know if his accounts go back online, okay? I don't use that stuff, so...

NATHAN. Um, sure.

(**NATHAN** *types into his phone.*)

TRISH. Why don't you go to him?

NATHAN. Jeremy?

TRISH. No, Austin. If he can't come here, why don't you go to him?

NATHAN. No, it's not... It's a delicate situation where he's staying.

TRISH. Have you tried calling him instead of just texting?

NATHAN. I really don't want to talk about him anymore. I know you mean well –

TRISH. I just – I learned the hard way what you can lose by letting people go.

NATHAN. You can't actually hold on to people.

TRISH. You have to try.

NATHAN. It's not always your decision. Or theirs. People can get taken, ya know?

TRISH. What happened to your father –

NATHAN. Was nothing he deserved. Nothing any of us deserved. But someone could just do that to him. They didn't care. None of us got any say in it.

TRISH. That's not the case with Austin. You do have a say. Fight for him!

(**NATHAN** *looks at her for a moment, not unkindly.*)

NATHAN. Do you want me to give you Jeremy's number?

(**TRISH** *looks at* **NATHAN**, *considers his offer.*)

TRISH. No, I already have it. I don't need it.

(**LIZ** *re-enters. Her appearance has once again slightly changed.*)

LIZ. Nathan, have you seen my portable radio?

(**TRISH** *sees it, and moves to point out its location.*)

NATHAN. No. It's not in your bedroom?

LIZ. No.

(**TRISH** *stops. She looks back and forth between the radio,* **LIZ** *and* **NATHAN**. *She says nothing.*)

NATHAN. Are you sure?

LIZ. It's not in there. I need to switch out the batteries tonight.

NATHAN. Did you accidentally pack it in with the supplies *again*?

LIZ. I only did that one time!

NATHAN. Twice just last week.

LIZ. Let me know if you come across it in here? I'll double check the bins.

(**LIZ** *exits again.* **TRISH** *turns to* **NATHAN**.)

TRISH. It's right there!

NATHAN. I know.

TRISH. So why didn't you say something?

NATHAN. Why didn't *you* say something?

TRISH. I was going to, but then you said it wasn't there and I got confused. I thought maybe there was some reason you were telling her it wasn't there.

NATHAN. Of course there's a reason. I hate that radio. It's loud and staticky and she won't ever play music. It's just people shouting crazy conspiracy theories all night long. She wants to hear the latest version of how the world's about to end so she can prioritize her supplies in the morning. That's the daily routine.

TRISH. She told me she got rid of the TV because of the news, and not wanting to get sucked in.

NATHAN. Yeah, she did.

TRISH. But she'll listen to it on the radio?

NATHAN. What she's listening to is not news. It's just chatter. She stays up all night with it.

TRISH. I don't know what to do here. How can I help you?

NATHAN. You can't. There's really nothing else to be done. Let's just enjoy a moment of peace.

TRISH. I miss the days of you and Jeremy playing in my backyard. At the time I thought you two were so *loud*. Running into the house, then out of the house. There were days when it felt like I would never get another moment of peace and quiet. I would've paid any amount of money for a few minutes where I could sit and hear my own thoughts. Now, it's only quiet. The grass is always greener, I guess.

NATHAN. I feel like the grass is kinda brown and dead on both sides of the fence, at this point.

TRISH. Oh, you can't think like that.

NATHAN. I miss that time too. Playing over at your place. We had fun.

TRISH. Jeremy was always a little shy and awkward when it came to talking with kids his own age. I don't know why. That's why I was happy you were close by and so friendly. You were always such a good friend to him.

NATHAN. But not... did you ever worry we were "too good" of friends?

TRISH. What?

NATHAN. Like, growing up, did you ever think that maybe we were too good of friends?

TRISH. Nathan, I've never thought poorly about you.

NATHAN. That's not what I –

TRISH. Nothing about you ever made me uncomfortable. Where did you get that idea?

NATHAN. Jeremy said you put a stop to our sleepovers. In Junior High. He said you didn't want us camping out together anymore.

> *(There is truth to this, but* **TRISH** *can't believe she ever said those words so blatantly to Jeremy.)*

TRISH. That's... I don't know what he... Well, there was *one* time he asked and I said no, but that was about his grades. He was not focusing and I kept telling him if we didn't see improvement he wasn't going to any parties, or having people stay over, or any other special privileges. But I never said, "Never again," about you. I can't believe he said that.

NATHAN. Don't worry about it. It's fine.

TRISH. I was happy he had a friend as good as you. And if anyone thought otherwise, they just didn't have their facts in order. That's all.

(A thought occurs to **NATHAN.***)*

NATHAN. Oh! You know what? I cleaned out my closet the other day so Mom could use it for more space and I found a box of stuff I salvaged after Prudence. There was something of Jeremy's in there. You should have it.

TRISH. What is it? No, it doesn't matter. You should keep it.

NATHAN. Hold on, I'll go get it. I'll at least show you. It's little. You might want it.

> *(He exits into the hallway.* **TRISH** *stands alone in the room. She pours herself more wine, drinks it down quickly. Pours again. Sips more slowly. We hear the sound of plaster crumbling from within the wall behind the oven.* **TRISH** *listens for it. It sounds like an animal burrowing.)*

TRISH. What is that – mice? Oh, don't be mice...

> *(***TRISH** *approaches the wall. The crumbling sound intensifies. It sounds like tiny claws are scraping away, digging their way out from the inside.* **TRISH** *touches the wall and it stops. She removes her hand from the wall and the clawing starts again. She puts her hand back, and it stops. She hears a new sound. It is the rubbing of a hand against glass on the window against the upstage wall. The drawn curtains in front of the window prevent* **TRISH** *from seeing who is there. She approaches the curtains. The sound stops. She pulls the curtains open. The window pane is foggy with breath. A light comes on from outside. We see there is a message written in capital letters on the window that says, "COME HOME, TRISH!" with a smiley face beneath it.)*

No! NO!

> (**TRISH** *pulls the curtains shut tight again.
> She staggers back, bumping into the table,
> knocking some chess pieces over. We hear the
> scraping sound from the walls again, as the
> lights flicker.* **TRISH** *cowers on the ground.
> Light shines up through the floorboards. The
> flickering lights dance across the kitchen
> toward the hallway.* **LIZ** *and* **NATHAN** *are
> standing in the hallway entrance, looking
> at* **TRISH** *in shock. They are both wearing
> "I Survived The Nuclear Winter" t-shirts. The
> lights return to normal.)*

Sixth Escalation

LIZ. Trish! What happened?

> (**NATHAN** *runs over to help* **TRISH** *up. She
> tries to crawl further away from the window.)*

TRISH. He's here. Liz, he's here!

LIZ. Austin?

TRISH. No, the man who was in my house! He's come over
here now. I told you he would.

LIZ. There is no one else here.

TRISH. Outside. At the window. He was writing a message
to me. He knew my name.

LIZ. That's not possible.

TRISH. Look! Please!

> (**LIZ** *goes to the window and pulls back the
> curtain. There are boards along the glass
> from the outside.)*

LIZ. We've got storm boards up. The glass is protected. See?

TRISH. What?

LIZ. It must've been a trick of the light or something.

TRISH. I heard his fingers against the glass.

LIZ. It was probably wind in the trees.

TRISH. Wind in the –

LIZ. You see the boards, right?

TRISH. Yes.

LIZ. There's no message, is there?

TRISH. No. But –

LIZ. Maybe that's enough wine. We should switch you over to coffee. I'll start a pot.

TRISH. You don't –

(**LIZ** *notices the portable radio.*)

LIZ. Oh, here's my radio!

TRISH. Yes, there it is. I was going to tell you it was there.

LIZ. Well, thanks for your help. I left the batteries in my room. Nathan, start the coffee. We'll have it with the pie.

(**LIZ** *exits with the radio.* **NATHAN** *starts putting chess pieces back on the board as* **TRISH** *collects herself.*)

TRISH. I like to think of myself as a calm, rational person.

NATHAN. I get it. I like to think of myself as six-foot-three.

(*He smiles at her.*)

TRISH. This is serious. Whoever it is, they're about to make a move. We have to get out of here.

NATHAN. Mom won't leave.

TRISH. We have to convince her. We'll make a run for my car. It's already on the street. We'll get in and pull away before whoever-it-is can get in front of us.

NATHAN. I know you're freaked out, but no one's gonna get in here. You gotta try to breathe and relax. Here. This is what I went to get for you.

(**NATHAN** *hands an action figure to* **TRISH**.)

TRISH. A G.I. Joe?

NATHAN. Yeah. Technically, he was with Cobra. The bad guys. He was my favorite character on the show and a Limited Edition figure. Hard to find. But you bought him for Jeremy and Jeremy gave him to me. So I'm giving him back to you.

TRISH. No, you should keep him, if he's your favorite. Jeremy had so many of these guys. I'm sure I have a whole box of them in the house still.

NATHAN. I just thought you –

TRISH. Are you still missing any pieces that I knocked over?

NATHAN. Just the red king. He seems to have rolled away.

TRISH. Oh, I know.

(*She places the action figure in the red king's place. The light above the table flickers, as a darkness flickers in* **NATHAN**.)

He can fill in until the true king returns.

NATHAN. Alright. Have it your way.

(*He fiddles with the G.I. Joe. The light above the table flickers.* **NATHAN** *smiles.*)

Would you play a game with me?

TRISH. Oh, I think I've had too much wine to think two steps ahead at this point. You'd beat me right away!

NATHAN. No, not chess. It's more of a riddle game. It's called, "Two Lies and a Truth."

TRISH. Don't you mean, "Two Truths and a Lie?"

NATHAN. No, I meant it how I said it. Someone comes up with two big lies and one unthinkable truth and the other person tries to figure out what the truth is.

TRISH. I'm not very good with making up lies.

NATHAN. You just have to be good at seeing the truth. I'll go first with the three statements and you try to guess which one's real. Okay?

TRISH. Okay.

NATHAN. Okay. Statement One. You, Trish, don't have a house. You don't have a job. You are not really friends with my mom. You are just one of this town's many homeless crazy people, living out of an abandoned car.

TRISH. That's *one* statement?

NATHAN. There's a little more. Every so often you come by here, warning us about a shadowy man who's waiting for you, "in your house." We calm you down and then you're back on your way. Okay, that's all of Statement One.

TRISH. Well, after all that I can't imagine what Statement Two could be!

NATHAN. Statement Two: I was the person you saw in your bedroom window tonight. I got off work, went to the store to pick up the groceries for Mom, and when I came back, I saw that the lights were off in your house. Your car wasn't in the driveway. And I was... curious. It'd been a long time since I'd been inside. I wondered if it still looked like rich people lived there. I guessed that you still kept an extra key in the planter by the downstairs window and that the alarm was still Jeremy's birthday. First, I went upstairs into

Jeremy's room. It's weird, there's nothing of his left in there but the air still kinda smells like him, you know? I lied down on his bed. Jerked off. Cleaned up. Went into your room, which is kind of a mess. Bed not made. Dirty plates and food wrappers mixed in with the sheets. Then I walked to your window and just stood there. Waiting.

TRISH. Why?

NATHAN. I became fascinated by the perspective. I imagined you standing there, looking down at the rest of the world. Feeling safe and above it all. Even alone in a big house, I bet it feels good to have that perch. I waited so that I could see what you looked like from up there. I wanted you to see me with our positions reversed. When you drove up, I saw you jump out of the car and come over to our house. Once I saw you were inside, I followed.

TRISH. I see now what you're doing with this incredibly creepy game.

NATHAN. You do?

TRISH. Yes. You have presented these two stories that are so awful and unbelievable that when the third statement you present me with is sensible and true, I'll understand how unrealistic my original fears were. For the record, the code to my house is not Jeremy's birthday. I turned his room into a workout space and my bedroom is spotless. I never have food in bed. Not even a cup of coffee.

NATHAN. I guess you figured me out.

TRISH. So now you've given me the two lies. What's the truth?

NATHAN. Statement Three... I poisoned the pie.

TRISH. What?

NATHAN. That's why I've been telling you to leave. It's not meant for you. It's for Mom and me. I mixed in some of the stronger pills she's been collecting. We're gonna eat the pie, fall asleep, and never wake up.

TRISH. That's a third lie.

NATHAN. No. We can't live like this anymore. We don't have a future. So tonight, it's good night and goodbye. Please go.

TRISH. You expect me to believe you'd just throw away your life this way? Or her life? Why would you even *say* something like that? That's the most terrible thing you've said!

NATHAN. I'm trying to explain – you weren't supposed to be here tonight!

TRISH. You're lying! You're trying to say anything you can think of to get me to leave, but... If you *did* really do something to that pie, you better throw it in the garbage right now. You have everything to live for.

NATHAN. Austin's leaving me. And I don't blame him. All night long, I've been trying to write him my goodbye letter. I need him to understand that it's just not possible for me to choose him over her. Even if I want to so much, I can't!

TRISH. It doesn't have to be either/or. You just have to talk to her. She doesn't see what this is costing you. She likes him. She wants to see him. She keeps saying so!

NATHAN. He doesn't want to see her.

TRISH. We have to get her out of this house. We have to work together. Don't you see?

NATHAN. There's no helping her. So I'm putting an end to it as peacefully as possible.

TRISH. You couldn't have poisoned the pie. You couldn't have. I don't believe it.

NATHAN. Well, I gave you three statements. Two lies and a truth. If the third one is a lie, then –

> (**TRISH** *reaches and knocks the G.I. Joe off its place on the chessboard. The light overhead flickers.* **NATHAN** *is sad, but nicer again.*)

Please go home. You don't actually care what happens to us anyway. You never did.

TRISH. Jeremy, that's not true!

NATHAN. I'm *Nathan*.

TRISH. Yes. Sorry. I know. Nathan, I –

> (*A high-pitched radio static fills the air.* **LIZ** *enters clutching the radio, her clothing slightly changed.*)

Seventh Escalation

LIZ. I replaced the batteries, but now I can't seem to get any of the stations to come in.

NATHAN. So shut it off.

LIZ. I didn't mess with the knobs. You think they all went off the air?

NATHAN. No, I just think that's a shitty radio.

LIZ. Watch your language... I like this one. It's easy to carry around.

NATHAN. Off now? Please?

> (**LIZ** *turns it off.*)

LIZ. Just for you. So, is the pie ready for us? Are *we* ready for the *pie*?

NATHAN. I am. Trish isn't going to stay, though.

LIZ. Oh, come on now.

TRISH. I'll stay. I'm just not feeling very hungry.

LIZ. Well, sober up with some coffee and we'll see how things go. Did you put it on yet?

NATHAN. You filled the giant thermos with coffee this morning. We can drink that.

LIZ. You could've made some fresh.

> (**LIZ** *goes to the counter and gets the thermos.* **NATHAN** *moves the chessboard to a stack of boxes by the door. He grabs a nearby hoodie and puts it on.*)

TRISH. It's my fault. We got to talking.

LIZ. About what?

NATHAN. The meaning of truth.

LIZ. Wow. Sorry I missed *that*.

> (**NATHAN** *and* **TRISH** *help set the table.* **LIZ** *tries the radio again. Again it makes an awful whining staticky sound.*)

NATHAN. Omigod, enough already!

> (*He tries to take the radio from her.*)

LIZ. I just want to find a station!

NATHAN. I'll find you a station later. I just don't want to listen to it right now. We're *talking*.

LIZ. Fine.

> (**LIZ** *lets* **NATHAN** *have the radio and he turns it off.* **LIZ** *picks up the pie from its resting place.*)

TRISH. You should get an XM satellite radio. Clearer signal and so many channel options.

LIZ. This one is free and it has all the shows I like on it.

> (**LIZ** *sets the pie down on the table.*)

Here we are! Looks gorgeous. Serve the coffee, Nathan.

NATHAN. It's right there on the table.

LIZ. So serve it. Drink up, Trish.

> (**NATHAN** *pours coffee in a mug for* **TRISH**.)

NATHAN. How 'bout you? You want any?

LIZ. Sure, I'll take a cup too. Let me get a knife for this.

NATHAN. Smells good, right?

LIZ. Smells good. Looks good. You should take a "SnapPhoto" of it and send it to Austin before I cut into it. Or would it be better after I cut it so it's a delicious slice of pie?

NATHAN. *SnapPhoto?*

LIZ. Whatever you call it.

NATHAN. Pass. Just cut and serve, please.

> (**LIZ** *cuts into the pie. The inside is a thick gooey red.*)

LIZ. Gorgeous!

> (**LIZ** *puts a slice on a plate and passes it to* **NATHAN**.)

NATHAN. Thanks.

> (**LIZ** *cuts another piece. Offers it to* **TRISH**.)

LIZ. You're sure?

> (**TRISH** *shakes her head.*)

Fine, I'll take this one. Don't wait for me, Nathan. Dig in.

NATHAN. No, you first. Tell me how you like it.

> (**LIZ** *sits. She takes a big forkful of pie and eats it. She smooshes it around inside her mouth, savoring the taste before she swallows.*)

LIZ. Mmmm! It's incredible.

NATHAN. Really?

LIZ. Perfection. I don't know how you get this kind of taste out of canned ingredients. Try it!

> (**NATHAN** *takes a big bite out of his own slice.*)

NATHAN. Oh man!

LIZ. I wasn't kidding.

NATHAN. You were not.

> (**TRISH** *watches them eat with silent dread. She wants to warn* **LIZ**, *but cannot bring herself to do it.*)

LIZ. Trish, you gotta get in on this.

TRISH. Later...maybe...

LIZ. Tell me: are you seeing anyone right now?

TRISH. Like a psychiatrist?

LIZ. No! Like a boyfriend!

TRISH. Oh! No. Definitely, no.

NATHAN. What about a psychiatrist?

LIZ. Nathan!

NATHAN. Because that's more invasive than asking about her love life?

LIZ. I was not being invasive. I was just thinking about it.

TRISH. Well, no to both. No boyfriends. No psychologists.

NATHAN. Psychiatrists.

TRISH. No men at all.

NATHAN. Women can be psychiatrists.

>   (**NATHAN** *puts his fork in his mouth and
>   slowly licks off all the cherry filling on it.*)

LIZ. Hey, what does your sister do at night?

TRISH. Hmm?

LIZ. Gladys. How does she get by at night?

TRISH. She does the same things any of us do, I guess.
   She's not bedridden. She can still maneuver herself
   around. We talk on the phone sometimes.

>   (*This doesn't sit right with* **LIZ**.)

LIZ. Huh...

NATHAN. Mom?

LIZ. I just had a thought of her sitting by herself at night
   and it made me sad.

>   (**LIZ** *takes another bite of pie. Swallows.*
>   **NATHAN** *also continues eating.*)

TRISH. She's okay. She...

LIZ. Nathan, try to find us some music on the radio.

NATHAN. When I'm done eating.

LIZ. I want us to have some upbeat music. I brought the
   energy down.

TRISH. You didn't. Nathan was telling me earlier how
   much you like listening to the nighttime shows.

NATHAN. I said you listen to it all night.

LIZ. I keep it on so I don't have to listen to you shout in
   your sleep!

NATHAN. I don't shout in my –

LIZ. Yes, you do. Your father was the same way. Always chattering away as soon as his head hit the pillow. I used to think that they were actually talking to each other. One would shout gibberish and then the other, taking turns. You guys should've talked to each other so much when you were awake.

> (**NATHAN** *drops his fork on his plate.* **LIZ** *regrets what she said.*)

I mean... I was actually a little jealous to be left out, and be kept awake by it. And you still shout on your own. I don't know if you're still shouting to him or someone else.

TRISH. Are you? Still shouting to him?

NATHAN. I don't know... Last night my dream was really crazy. I had written this huge book. Not like a novel. It was like an historical biography or something. It was all done and I was so proud of it. Then Dad was there next to me and he told me there were a lot of changes to it that needed to be made. I told him it was too late, but when I looked at the book again he'd made all these marks on every page, some in black ink, some in red and that was my only copy. I started *screaming* at him, how he had no business touching my things and he had ruined all my work. I couldn't stop screaming. I got so physically upset by it, that I shook myself awake. Isn't that nuts?

LIZ. It's like that every night with you.

TRISH. Nothing like that ever happened between you two in real life, did it?

NATHAN. That I wrote an historical biography? Um, definitely not!

LIZ. I'm just amazed you can remember your dreams at all. I never do.

TRISH. Never?

LIZ. Never in my life. I just close my eyes, then nothing, then I wake up.

TRISH. You're lucky. When I was little I used to have this one terrible recurring dream.

(**LIZ** and **NATHAN** continue to eat as she talks.)

I'd be riding bikes with my sister and we'd come up to our house, but instead of its normal colors, the whole house was painted in different shades of red. Everything – the siding, the shutters, the front door. And Gladys and I would go inside and there'd be all these witches and demons right in our living room having a birthday party. There were streamers and balloons and a punch bowl. No one paid attention to us. They were all laughing and running around the house. But also, in the middle of my sister's bedroom there was this grey man standing totally still while everyone danced around him. His stillness was the scariest part, because I knew any second he'd be ready to grab me, and if he did, I'd just get wrapped up inside of him and never get free. I wanted to get out of there before anyone noticed us, but they grabbed Gladys and took her down to the basement. And I couldn't get her back, so I'd run out the front door, I'd get back on my bike and pedal away, telling myself that was not my house.

I was just in a town that looked like mine, but it wasn't mine, and if I could just get back to the real town, then my real house would be there and Gladys would be waiting there too. And we'd be safe.

(**LIZ** begins using her hands to eat the pie. Her fingers and mouth are smeared with the red filling.)

NATHAN. Did you ever actually get there? In the dream?

TRISH. Sometimes. But sometimes no matter how hard I'd try, I just came back to the version of my house that was painted red.

LIZ. You've got a weird thing about houses.

(*She puts her plate down on the table.*)

I made a mess. I'm all sticky.

NATHAN. You've been enjoying that pie!

LIZ. I need a WetNap.

(**LIZ** *stands up to go to the kitchen cabinets.*)

NATHAN. They're all in the bathroom medicine cabinet.

LIZ. There should always be a box in the kitchen.

NATHAN. I *know*. I didn't replace the empty one. *I know*. I'm sorry.

LIZ. This is why I have to double check everything every day.

NATHAN. I'll go get you one.

LIZ. I can handle it.

(*She points at* **TRISH**.)

You. Cut yourself a piece of that pie. It's delicious. I'll consider it an insult if you don't try it. Alright?

TRISH. Sure.

LIZ. Do it now.

(**LIZ** *exits through the hall.* **TRISH** *picks up the knife.* **NATHAN** *watches her with anticipation.* **TRISH** *feels cornered. She is sure the pie is poisoned. She meets* **NATHAN**'s *gaze and gets an idea. She puts the blade against her open palm and cuts her hand deeply. She cries out in pain.* **NATHAN** *jumps up from his chair in shock.*)

Eighth Escalation

LIZ. *(Offstage.)* Trish?

NATHAN. Omigod!

> (**LIZ** *comes running back in, wearing her original outfit.*)

LIZ. What happened?

TRISH. The knife slipped as I was cutting into the pie!

LIZ. Let me see! Is it bad?

TRISH. It's bleeding. It really hurts!

LIZ. Come with me to the sink. Nathan, grab me the first aid kit on the top shelf in the hallway closet. We're gonna start by washing it out right now.

> (**NATHAN** *exits to get the kit.*)

TRISH. I'm afraid to open my hand. I don't want to look at it.

LIZ. Just close your eyes then, and let me put it under the water.

> (**LIZ** *turns on the faucet and* **TRISH** *cries out in shock as we hear the sound of rushing water from the sink.* **NATHAN** *re-enters with the kit. He is back wearing his first change of clothes.*)

NATHAN. What do you need?

LIZ. Antibiotic spray and the bandage, please.

TRISH. The cut's deep, isn't it?

LIZ. It's not that deep. I've got you. Here.

> (*The water stops.* **LIZ** *sprays the wound.*)

TRISH. It stings!

LIZ. It's going to. Apply pressure... Wrap it up... Press the thumb of your good hand right here. Elevate it. Nathan, get me an ice pack from the fridge.

> (**NATHAN** *gets an ice pack from the freezer as* **LIZ** *and* **TRISH** *move to sit at the table.*)

Let's just sit like this for a while, okay? You're going to be fine.

TRISH. No, I think I need to go to the emergency room. Drive me to Good Samaritan. It's not far.

LIZ. *Good Sam?* Honey, why don't I just amputate your hand right now and save the hospital bills?

TRISH. I'm not joking!

LIZ. Neither am I. That place has been falling apart for years. I'm not taking you there.

TRISH. But if I need stitches...

LIZ. You go to any ER this time of night, you'll just be sitting there waiting to be seen until morning anyway. Just keep it bandaged for now.

TRISH. Liz, you need to get out of this house!

LIZ. Why?

TRISH. You've been poisoned.

LIZ. What?

TRISH. Nathan poisoned the pie!

> (**LIZ** *stares at her astounded.*)

He poisoned it. He just told me.

LIZ. When?

TRISH. While he was mixing the ingredients.

LIZ. No! When did he *tell you* he poisoned the pie?

TRISH. When you were in the other room.

LIZ. He said, "I poisoned the pie," and you responded by slicing your hand open?

TRISH. No, earlier tonight. You were getting the batteries, and –

LIZ. He told you before I served the pie.

TRISH. Yes.

LIZ. And then you sat there and watched us eat the pie.

TRISH. Yes.

LIZ. And you never thought to say, "Liz, don't eat that poisoned pie"?

TRISH. I *did* think to say it!

LIZ. Then why didn't you?

TRISH. I wasn't sure it was poisoned then!

LIZ. But NOW you're sure?

TRISH. Liz, please. We have to get to the hospital. There might not be much time.

LIZ. I'm not going anywhere. Neither are you.

> (*She takes her fork, digs it into the rest of the pie, and points the fork toward* **TRISH***'s face.*)

Eat it.

TRISH. What?

LIZ. Put this in your mouth and chew.

TRISH. I can't!

> (**LIZ** *puts the fork in her own mouth. She digs into the pie again and shovels more into her mouth. She points the fork toward* **TRISH** *again.*)

LIZ. Come on!

TRISH. Liz, please stop!

LIZ. What is wrong with you? The pie is fine!

TRISH. But he told me... We were playing two truths and a – two *lies* and a truth and he...

LIZ. You were playing what?

TRISH. The other things can't be true. This is what's real!

(**LIZ** *turns to* **NATHAN**.)

LIZ. What did you say to her?

NATHAN. I was just trying to get her to go home. I didn't think she'd hurt herself!

LIZ. You and I will talk about this later.

TRISH. There isn't going to be a later if we don't get both of you to a doctor right now.

LIZ. Will you stop? Nathan was making it all up. It's not true.

TRISH. Why would he make something like that up?

LIZ. He was probably worried that the longer you stayed, the likelier it would be that I'd go off on you, and he wanted to spare you that. He's got a soft spot for you.

TRISH. What?

LIZ. It's always been that way. You're the mom who could provide all the toys, all the goodies. Giant swing sets and in-ground pools! Some of us didn't inherit money and then go on to marry rich for extra cushion. Some of us worked just to make ends meet. We couldn't splurge on every indulgence. Hell, I'd want you as my mom too.

NATHAN. That's not how it was.

LIZ. No, I get it. And it was nice that you always made him feel included. It was. He's still very protective of those memories. And of you. That's what this is.

TRISH. No. There's more going on here than you realize.

LIZ. Oh?

TRISH. I know about how you won't leave the house. I know the whole story.

LIZ. Wow, you know the "whole story?" Is that right, *neighbor*?

TRISH. I know you need help. I know Nathan needs –

LIZ. Don't talk to me about my son's needs.

TRISH. You're robbing him of his future! You don't even know it!

LIZ. I am? A minute ago you were warning me that he was robbing me of mine! Which is it?

TRISH. Both!

LIZ. You're confused. You don't know what you're talking about.

TRISH. When was the last time you stepped outside this house? Tell me.

LIZ. I don't know. I don't want to go outside. What's the problem with that?

TRISH. The problem is you've given up on yourself.

NATHAN. Please just go, Trish.

LIZ. No! And no, I have not given up on myself. My world has gotten smaller. So what? That's life. Your world starts out small, then it expands and then it contracts again. When our kids were younger, my world was bigger by necessity. I had to be out doing things with him. Now, as I get older, my world shrinks again. The outside world doesn't need me. May it go on spinning into chaos on its own. I'm fine with that.

TRISH. You're not fine. You can't live like this.

LIZ. Why not? I can do everything from home. What am I missing out on?

TRISH. What about *people*?

LIZ. *People?* What is so great about people? What kind of *people* do I need? People like you?

NATHAN. Mom. We don't have to do –

TRISH. Why not people like me?

LIZ. Oh, where to start?

TRISH. You know, I don't deserve to be continually insulted just because –

LIZ. You're the one intruding on our lives. We didn't ask for you to come over tonight. Why on Earth did you come *here* looking for help, anyway?

TRISH. I saw you were home. You were the closest person –

LIZ. And proximity won out over decency, huh?

TRISH. How is reaching out for help considered indecent?

LIZ. You haven't stepped foot in this house since the day of Joe's funeral. And that whole day you didn't say a damn thing to me. Richard did all the talking. That's what a friend does? Where were you when I could have really used somebody? I'd been there for you at your lowest moment! Something you seem all too happy to have forgotten.

TRISH. I wanted to be there for you, I did, but I –

LIZ. *It was you and me.* We shared our whole lives as our kids grew up. Then Joe died, and you completely pulled away. Why?

TRISH. I didn't know what to say to you.

LIZ. Why not try, "Sorry for your loss! Anything I can do, please tell me! I'm right next door! I'm here for you!" That's so hard?

TRISH. I couldn't. I couldn't say anything. I was too ashamed.

LIZ. Ashamed of what?

TRISH. Don't make me say it.

LIZ. You can say it, or you can eat this fucking pie! Those are your options. Now, I'm tired of the nonsense. Why were you so ashamed?

TRISH. Because I was happy. When I first heard what happened to Joe, when I knew he was gone...the first thing I felt was joy. Not shock. Not grief. Those things came later, they did. But right in that moment... I was excited that I never had to feel lesser than you again. Is that what you need me to say?

LIZ. Lesser than me.

TRISH. I hadn't been happy in a very long time. I should've been, but I wasn't. Not with Richard, not with Jeremy, not with the house or anything. And you and Joe really were happy. Looking at you together, it was undeniable. I hated it. And I hated myself for being jealous, but it consumed me. Every day I hoped that something would happen to drive you two the tiniest bit apart. Not that one of you would die, just *something* so you wouldn't be so damn happy together all the time. So you could feel how I'd been feeling.

LIZ. So when you heard what happened to him, how he was *violated* and left for dead on the side of the road, how our family was torn apart – you felt good about that?

TRISH. And I felt so sick over it. I mean, how could I feel that way? For years, I'd been secretly wishing misery on my best friend and now here it was, in the most awful permanent way. It was a nightmare. I couldn't face it. I couldn't face you. I couldn't share my shame with anyone. So I stayed away.

LIZ. That must've been *so difficult* for you. To carry *such* a burden? *Oh*, if only I had *known*!

TRISH. No, this is why I was never going to tell you. Words can't express it. They can't.

LIZ. Oh, I'm sure staying quiet about your disgusting desire for my unhappiness was much more convenient.

TRISH. It wasn't convenient at all!

LIZ. You know what really pisses me off? The people that I've loved in my life and lost? They were all taken from me. Everyone you've lost, you just let slip away. You let your whole family walk right out the front door.

TRISH. That's not true. I didn't let my family go.

LIZ. Then you drove them away. Bye, Gladys! Bye, Richard! Bye, Jeremy! What does that say about you, Trish? It's not very flattering.

TRISH. I'd rather be alone right now than live here like you do.

LIZ. Is that so? Well, I'm sorry my life is such a disappointment to you. Thanks for coming over and filling in some blanks for me. Very illuminating. Now the door's right there. I'm happy to give you some pie to go, if you want. No need to return the Tupperware. A parting gift from me to you.

> (**LIZ** *gets Tupperware, scoops some pie in it and slams it down in front of* **TRISH**.)

TRISH. I want to leave you with something too. You wanted my truth? Well, I gave it to you, but now I want you to see your own truth.

LIZ. And what's that, in your opinion?

TRISH. You've turned your house into a prison. Not just for you, but for Nathan.

LIZ. Nathan is not a prisoner here.

TRISH. That's how you make him feel. He's given up everything for you.

NATHAN. Don't put words in my mouth.

LIZ. He can go at anytime. We're happy here. He wants to stay.

TRISH. No, he doesn't. You've trapped him. He's not going to abandon you. He'd rather give up a chance at his own happiness than leave you here alone while everything falls apart.

NATHAN. Don't speak for me. Fight about your own problems. Leave me out of it.

TRISH. Austin left him because of you.

LIZ. What?

NATHAN. Mom, that's not true.

TRISH. Yes, it is. Austin didn't want to be in this house because of you and he couldn't stay where he was and Nathan couldn't leave you, so that was that. You need to know that.

LIZ. Did Austin really –

NATHAN. No, we're spending the whole day together tomorrow. We are! Mom, she's nuts... She doesn't... Don't listen to her. She's... Mom, please.

(**LIZ** *knows it's true.* **NATHAN** *gives up.*)

TRISH. What's the point of all this, Liz? What's the point of all these supplies stored around the house? What's the point of surviving if you don't want to actually live?

LIZ. What do you know about it? You have the luxury of making decisions like that while the rest of us are just one tragedy away from being completely wiped out. Yeah, I'm trying to keep us alive. Who else am I supposed to rely on? Not you.

TRISH. When did you ever reach out and I smacked your hand away? You say I haven't shown up on your doorstep in seven years? Well when's the last time you showed up on mine? If you weren't too proud to ask for help –

LIZ. Too proud? I wish I was too proud. I wish I had never lowered myself to ask for help from someone like you, but I did it for my son and it still came to nothing.

TRISH. When?

LIZ. Hurricane Prudence.

TRISH. What about it?

LIZ. Our house was flooded that night. The whole rest of the street was flooded, but the water never crept up to your house, did it? That little hill your house sits on makes a great deal of difference when the sea level rises. What else could I do? I grabbed Nathan and we made our way over to your house.

TRISH. *During the storm?*

LIZ. During the storm. The whole night was pitch black, but the lights were on in your place. I thought, "Thank god, she has that generator! Thank god, she's home!" I pounded on your door. I screamed – begged – for you to let us in. You wouldn't open the door for us.

TRISH. I didn't know! I couldn't hear anything over the wind and the rain. I swear!

LIZ. I saw you. Standing in your bedroom window. A dark silhouette staring out into the night. And you saw me. I know you did. And what did you do? You closed the curtains and blocked out our only light.

TRISH. I never saw you through the storm. If I had, I would've let you in!

LIZ. I tried to believe that, as we waded through the water back to our house. That's what I told Nathan. But deep down I knew different. And tonight, you've admitted it. You acted shamefully toward me when Joe died and you acted shamefully again that night, hoping that the storm would wipe us out completely. Then there wouldn't be any unpleasant reminders left of what a horrible person you are.

TRISH. I'm not a horrible person. I'm a caring person.

LIZ. Who do you care about besides yourself? Who do you ever sacrifice for?

TRISH. My sister, for one.

LIZ. Your sister?

TRISH. I do. I take care of her.

LIZ. Who do you think you're talking to right now? You think I forgot what happened?

NATHAN. Mom...

LIZ. I let you in tonight to show you I'm the bigger person. After everything you did and everything you failed to do, I'd still open the door for you. I wanted you to know that. I didn't know when I let you in how wrapped up you were in the lies you've been telling yourself. I really pity you. This whole martyr fantasy you've constructed –

NATHAN. Ma, just leave it alone.

TRISH. Martyr fantasy? I take good care of my sister. It's hard work. It's exhausting, actually, but I do it because I love her. You don't know anything about her. Gladys was strong and beautiful and talented. She used to make these beautiful hand-painted porcelain figurines. She would sell them, and I helped her with the orders and... no, that's not right... she...

(The lights flicker. Only **TRISH** *notices.)*

LIZ. Where is she, Trish? Where do you really go to visit her?

NATHAN. Mom, please.

TRISH. She's safe in her home. I saw her today. I cleaned... I'm a good person. I'm a good sister.

LIZ. Trish...you drove your sister away fighting her over your mom's estate. She died the following year without you ever reconciling.

LIZ. You sat right over there at my old kitchen table and cried about it on my shoulder. I was there for you. I felt no pleasure at your misfortune. I thought it was a horrible shame.

TRISH. No. You're a liar. You're cruel. I came over looking for help and you've been twisting my head around this whole time. I don't deserve this! I tried to warn you. Someone got into my house. The same someone who's now trying to make their way in here. But you won't see it! You refuse! But, still, I tried. I'm a good neighbor. I'm good. I'm good.

NATHAN. Trish...

TRISH. And I'm a good mother. Mistakes were made. Sure. But... I should've gone elsewhere for help tonight. That's clear to me now. Let's leave it at that.

LIZ. If that's where you want to leave it.

> (**TRISH** *turns to face the door, and stops, frightened. The lights dim and flicker again. She begins to laugh.*)

NATHAN. Trish?

TRISH. Oh, I'm fine, Jeremy. It's just so silly! There was never anyone in my house. I just left the lights on. I got so worked up over nothing. I need to go home. No one needs to go with me. I'll be fine.

> (**LIZ** *turns her back on* **TRISH**.)

LIZ. Get home safe. Don't be a stranger.

TRISH. I'll come by again another day when it's not so late. Maybe then... Goodbye.

> (**TRISH** *opens the front door. As it swings inward, the* **GREY MAN** *is waiting with arms outstretched. He wraps* **TRISH** *in his embrace. Neither* **LIZ** *nor* **NATHAN** *sees this. The* **GREY**

MAN pulls **TRISH** *into the night and she does not resist. The door shuts behind them.* **LIZ** *considers* **NATHAN**.)

Final Escalation

LIZ. Are you upset with me?

NATHAN. Why would I be?

LIZ. I was unkind to her. At the end.

NATHAN. Well... Some of it...was a long time coming.

LIZ. I don't want you to give up on happiness. Your father wouldn't want that either. Don't be stuck here like me, or let people slip away from you, like Trish. You follow your love. Call Austin tomorrow. Make it right.

NATHAN. Okay.

(*He coughs and walks back to the table.*)

LIZ. You want some water?

(*She coughs, and walks to the fridge for a bottle of water.*)

NATHAN. No, I'm okay.

LIZ. All that arguing with Trish made my throat sore. I shouldn't have lost my temper. I should be more like Sister Prudence, God rest her soul.

(**LIZ** *drinks some water.*)

NATHAN. Do you love her?

LIZ. Who? Sister Prudence?

NATHAN. No, Trish. You were saying how much you'd shared together. Do you feel love for her?

LIZ. I don't even know her now. If I ever really did.

NATHAN. I just think it's crazy how someone can leave you or betray you, but you can still love them, you know? No matter what they do. You think that's possible, right?

(*He coughs again. He feels strange inside.*)

LIZ. You're not making sense. Go to sleep. It feels late all of a sudden. I'm tired. We'll sort all this out in the morning. C'mon. Let's go.

NATHAN. I just want to stay here.

LIZ. I'm gonna turn the radio on. Will you listen with me tonight?

NATHAN. Yeah, okay.

LIZ. You will?

NATHAN. I will. Sit here with me, Mom.

(**LIZ** *coughs again. She turns on the radio and plays with the knob. A song comes through. Perhaps it's an instrumental version of "Is That All There Is?"*)

LIZ. Honey, I found music on the radio! I found a station with music! I remember this one! What is it called? You know it. What is it?

NATHAN. Mom...

(**LIZ** *moves to him. His mind begins to spin.*)

---

* A license to produce *THE LIGHTS ARE ON* does not include a performance license for "Is That All There Is?" The publisher and author suggest that the licensee contact ASCAP or BMI to ascertain the music publisher and contact such music publisher to license or acquire permission for performance of the song. If a license or permission is unattainable for "Is That All There Is?", the licensee may not use the song in *THE LIGHTS ARE ON* but should create an original composition in a similar style or use a similar song in the public domain. For further information, please see the Music and Third-Party Materials Use Note on page iii.

LIZ. What's wrong, sweetheart?

NATHAN. I'm worried I'm going to slip into a nightmare.

LIZ. Just listen to the music.

(*The music becomes distorted and cuts out.*)

Oh, no. I have to replace the batteries again. I thought I just did that.

(*She coughs and collapses into the chair next to him. She feels strange, but happy.* **NATHAN** *watches her, anxious.*)

NATHAN. You're alright?

LIZ. I'm perfectly fine. What's got you so upset?

NATHAN. I'm worried Trish didn't make it home okay. I'm worried I'm going to dream about that forever.

LIZ. I bet she's walking up that hill right now, and... oh! You're not going to believe this, Nathan. I'm just remembering a beautiful dream I once had. I can't believe it. I never remember my dreams!

NATHAN. Tell it to me.

(**NATHAN** *turns to see the gun. With effort, he reaches for it.*)

LIZ. I'm outside. I'm standing on a hill. There's nothing blocking the view. I can see for miles. I can see anything I want. I can zoom in to see the tiniest blade of grass in exquisite detail. In high definition. And there's one tree on the hill. The old tree from our backyard. And you're climbing in the tree. And Jeremy is up there too. Or maybe it's Austin. Or I think they're both there.

(**NATHAN** *can't reach the gun. His arm falls. He rests his head on the table. Life drains from him.*)

LIZ. But even the tree doesn't block my view. I can see past the tree or see through it rather. And your father is there. He is barbecuing and the smoke is rising up to the clear blue sky.

> (**LIZ**'s *head starts to spin. The end comes rushing in.*)

And he's laughing at me about...something. Oh, Joe. And Trish is there with Richard on a picnic blanket. They're so happy...like I've never seen them before. We all are. I can see everything... It's a blessing to be together.

> (**LIZ** *stops talking and then stops breathing. She and* **NATHAN** *sit slumped into each other at the table, motionless. There is silence. Then a scratching sound comes from within the walls. All of the lights in the house turn on. The music from the radio comes back on. The scratching gets louder. In a last gasp from the house, the lights all flicker and then go out. The music stops.*)

End of Play

Printed in the USA
CPSIA information can be obtained
at www.ICGtesting.com
JSHW011428030924
69236JS00020B/452

9 780573 711275